For Casey

Straight Up

a Brazen Boys story

by Daryl Banner

Books By Daryl Banner

Straight Up: a Brazen Boys story

Cover & Interior Design : Daryl Banner

Cover Model : Nick Duffy
www.instagram.com/nickduffyfitness

Photo of Nick Duffy by Simon Barnes

Straight Up

a Brazen Boys story

by Daryl Banner

[1]

He throws me into the couch, then climbs atop me like a horse, straddling my chest and gripping my shirt tight.

It's finally going to happen.

He tells me he wants to have his way with me, his eyes greedy and black, all his dark hair tousled from our bout of wrestling on the floor where he almost tore my sleeve. Not that it matters, as I suspect my clothes won't be on for much longer at this rate.

I tell him I've always been his to do with as he pleases. He laughs in my face and, just when I think he's going to kiss me, he reaches down, slips his hand into my jeans and grabs a mighty handful of my manhood. I gasp, my lips parting, and an evil look of triumph takes his face.

This is mine, he tells me in a word or two. *This is mine until I'm done with you, Benny. You got that? Your cock belongs to me.*

Between stolen breaths, I tell him to do whatever he wants with it. My roommate of two years and best buddy of seven, I tell Trent I'm so fucking horny for him I feel sick.

Or maybe it's his vice grip on my balls that's inspiring the nausea. *You're goddamned right,* he whispers, then clasps my hair into his other hand and pulls my head back onto the couch. One hand gripping my junk, the other my hair, I'm in his complete control.

Just where I've always wanted to be for years. Ever since grade school when he started dating girls and I felt the stab of jealousy every time he brought one around. Ever since we enrolled at (and dropped out of) the same college and our parents called us "inseparable" and my sister rolled her eyes and said we had a bromance. Yeah, a bromance, a romance, every kind of mance, whatever kind, I want it all. Trent and his messy hair and his piercing eyes and his slender sculpted swimmer's body and his skinny jeans and his lip ring and about a hundred other things I could list about him.

I'm not sure how it happens, but suddenly his lips are an inch from mine. He smells so clean. He calls me something—*horny fuck, dipshit, my bitch, boy toy*, I don't quite hear him—and then he lets go of my hair and starts to unzip himself. Through the tattered skinny jeans, I see the outline of Trent's cock. Yes, it's big, I've seen it many times, though not in this context. And it is *raging*.

I can't believe this is happening. All these years ... why hasn't this happened yet? Why didn't I know that my own best friend ...?

Fuck face, I hear him say, though I don't see his mouth move. Those full lips and that lip ring and that look in his eyes ... Kiss me,

Trent. Stop being such a tease, please, and put those lips on me. Let me feel those lips, please. Don't make me beg.

Then he sits up and I get a front row seat to his pants opening. He's going commando today and his cock, throbbing and veiny, pops out and stares me in the face.

Little Trent: not so little at all.

He asks me if I want to suck it. Even with the courtesy of a question, I know I don't really have a choice. Not that I want or need one. I want that cock so far down my throat I gag. Please, please, please. Please let me have that cock. I open my mouth, ready, my tongue ready to receive, my hungry eyes watching.

You want it? The evil grin that spreads across his face makes my cock pulse. It's strange how he's let go of my balls, yet I feel like he's still got them squeezed with his long, mighty fingers. I want it so bad.

My mouth is open. Please, please, please.

All the times our hands would graze when we both reached into the chip bag. All the video games we'd play—how even the boyish competitiveness between us would somehow seem so sexual. All the times we'd borrow each other's clothes, even though I'm bulkier and his clothes fit hilariously tight on me.

Trent brings his hands up behind his head, all cocky-like, and just with his hips he thrusts himself at my mouth.

His cock slides in like a friend who's come home. My tongue, the welcome mat. I feel his weight on my chest as his thighs squeeze, pushing his cock in, deeper and deeper.

I moan, feeling his cock in my mouth, twisting my head and sucking. I hear him laugh, as if my horniness amuses him. There is something about the taste of his cock that intrigues me—something musky, masculine, sweaty. The scent and the taste reel me in, making my heart drum with excitement. I'm consumed by him. I'm engulfed in everything Trent, from his smell to his taste to his weight on my body.

"How's that taste, dumb fuck?"

I open my eyes.

"Tasty?" asks Trent again, and he's not straddling me. He was never straddling me. I was dreaming. His pants are zipped up and there's no cock in mouth.

I try to speak, find my mouth is stuffed. I reach up and pull out a sock—Trent's sock.

"What the fuck?" I say, half a laugh and half a repulsed choke bleating out of me.

"You were moaning and shit, I felt left out," answers Trent, amused. "What the fuck did you dream you had in your mouth? My cock?" He laughs, then adds: "Need a trip to the spank bank, Benny?"

I look down my body and realize I'm tenting in my sweat pants. My face flushes red, but I fight the humiliation and say back, "Yeah, alright, wanna tell me how long you were lookin' down at my boner like that, fag?"

He snorts. "I'm out. Catch you after work, bitch." Then he struts to the door.

I watch him as he leaves, how his ass and his tiny waist move in those skinny jeans and how his broad shoulders give him that athletic triangular shape. I'm breathing heavily as though my dream were real, watching hungrily as Trent shuts the door behind him.

But my dream will never be real. He doesn't know I'm into him. I'm just his best friend who's only dated two girls in my life. Trent will always be the straight roomie I can never have. I will always be the desperately lonely dude everyone thinks is straight, the man's man, the dude with the bulky football build who's never played a day of football in his life. It's only in my longing mind that these desires are fulfilled. If only it weren't for the agony of waking up ...

His sock still in my grasp, I cram it back in my mouth and slip a hand down my sweat pants. My eyes rocking back, I start jerking off and struggling frenziedly to return to my place on the couch, to the engorged cock on my tongue, to the weight of Trent atop me with his smart fingers and evil plans.

[2]

I told him it was a bad idea, but in typical Trent fashion, he did it anyway.

"You'll like her," he insists, slapping my tummy as he gets off the couch to grab another beer. "Wear somethin' snazzy, bro."

I scoff, annoyed, and return my attention to the game I'm playing, tapping buttons on the controller mindlessly. When Trent returns and passes in front of me, I'm distracted by his jeans hanging low, teasing me with more than just the waistband of his underwear, then find when my gaze returns to the TV that I'm being attacked and am nearing zero health. That's pretty much my life in a nutshell: always distracted by boys that I'm caught off-guard and drained to near-death by zombies.

"Tonight at seven," Trent tells me as he cracks open his can, "at the Kegs & Dregs."

"Ugh, I hate Kegs."

"She's way the fuck into you," he goes on, throwing an arm over the back of the couch. His fingers graze my neck. "Showed her that pic of you with the green background, told her you were the no-sex-'til-marriage type. That made her wet."

"Dude, that pic of me's almost five years old, from prom."

"You look the same. Go take a shower, get ready. I'm taking you."

My character dies and I grunt, tossing the controller into his lap, giving up. "Your turn. I'll take myself."

He takes it, starting the level over. "Gross, controller's sweaty. You can't take yourself, bro. I need the car tonight, so I'm dropping you early. Just call when you need to be picked up, or decide to go home with her, or fuck her in the unisex, whatever. You need to get laid, you're way too uptight."

I roll my eyes, cross my arms and sink into the couch, willing myself to disappear. His shoulder pushes into mine as he relaxes into the couch himself. Suddenly, my sourness is replaced by comfort, just with the subtle presence of his body against mine. It doesn't take much to make me happy, it really doesn't. Trent could make me so happy, if he only ...

"When you bone her," says Trent, "make sure you eat her out real good first, get her all nice and wet. And condom-up, dude, you don't want to splooge in her and have a little Benny running around our pad."

Way to spoil my passion, roomie. "Noted. What do you need the car for anyway?"

Trent smirks, sucking in his lips and squinting at the screen. I know that look.

"You're kidding me," I say flat out, giving him a shove from my shoulder. "I thought—"

"Her parents are gone for the weekend, so I gotta get as much ass as I can, bro." He sighs, likely because he feels my disapproving glare. "You saw the same pics of her house as I did, didn't you? She's fuckin' loaded."

"So's her daddy's shotgun," I spit back. "A girl you gotta tiptoe around parents to see is not a girl you can make it with. Especially when you got five years on her."

"Six." Trent swallows hard, mashes his fingers into the controller and narrows his eyes to practically slits.

I sigh, feeling equally annoyed with and sorry for my dummy roommate I'm in love with—or whatever. I don't even want to argue with him whether the girl he's trying to see is even legal. I have my own girl issues to worry about. What do I wear tonight? What outfit says: "Hello. I'm only going out with you because my roommate thinks I need to get laid, but I'm actually zero percent interested, to no fault of yours, as I'm, unbeknownst to roommate, a big horny virgin homo."

My roommate throws the controller across the room and hollers out in frustration. I stare at the "GAME OVER" on the screen with little zombie bites in it. Game's always over when it comes to me and craving anything with a dude. It's hopeless. It'll never happen. Maybe I should meet a girl I like enough and just do the husband-and-wife thing, have a few kids, coach the local soccer team. Pump enough self-denial into the marriage bed and just about anything can happen when the lights are out.

"I ain't ever gonna be happy," Trent groans, glaring at the screen.

Took the words outta my mouth.

[3]

She orders a tea with no lemon because lemons make her queasy. She decides she only wants a salad because she's got this goal of losing fifteen pounds by the fifteenth. Her name is Sandy and she's wearing something and her hair is some kind of color and blah, blah, blah.

"Are you alright?"

I lift my eyebrows. "Sorry?"

She nibbles at a forkful of greens with the daintiness of some princess, overlooking the massive burger and fries I ordered for myself with judgment. "You seem a bit preoccupied. I hope I'm not boring you."

"Not at all. Sorry, I didn't know I—"

"This was sprung on me too," she admits with a shrug, chewing. "If you'd rather just call it a night and, I don't know, meet up another time maybe, I'm just fine and dandy with that."

Her Texan accent is thick and borderline annoying, if it weren't for the fact that she's so damn nice. Actually, her niceness is annoying too. I don't want to be here.

"Nah, it's alright," I say instead after struggling to swallow a stale fry. I hate Kegs & Dregs. I hate everything. "We're here, so ..."

"Trent told me you work in sales?"

I roll my eyes. "What he means by that is, I'm a retail clerk. Lame, I know, but it's just a day job until I get the chance to do what I really want."

"And that's ...?"

"Take over my pop's business," I answer after swallowing a bite of dried-out burger. I really, really hate Kegs. "He's got a store off Stoneridge and Fourth. I always wanted to own my own store, call the shots."

"You like being in charge?"

"Usually." I throw back my Coke. Even that's flat. *I fucking hate Kegs.*

I hear her moan. When I look up, I find her face wrinkled in disgust, staring across the room. I turn, following her line of sight.

The likely capturer of her attention is the local gay. Poor fool is all on his own on the dance floor, wagging his ass and flinging his arms around like four pinwheels. He is such a faggy McFaggerson. Dressed in a skin-tight yellow shirt with some angel-looking thing on the front and pants that he probably pulled from a woman's rack at Macy's, he dances all alone to the pop country music that's pumping the bar tonight. He's basically "the gay guy in town". If I talked to him, I'm one hundred percent sure I'd get at least a blowjob. I could have my gay cherry popped, just like that.

So why does he bother me so much?

Just in this moment, he turns around, his eyes connecting with mine. We went to school together, even though we never talked, but when he looks at me, he seems almost startled. Then a twisty sort of smile happens on his face and, as if inspired by my watching him, he dances with even more vigor than before. It's like I'm paying witness to some sort of gay mating ritual. This weird peacock is trying to wake little Benny between my thighs. He's not yet successful.

"I don't know why he comes here," my date Sandy says after sipping her no-lemon water. "No one wants him around."

Despite finding the flamer annoying as a fly in my dinner and never having had a thing to do with him in my life, I'm struck with a sudden desire to defend the little shit. "He's out there, but he ain't hurtin' no one."

"He's hurtin' my eyes." She rolls said eyes, then fixes them on me, smiling. "Trent said you were old-fashioned. I love an old-fashioned boy. You seem awful sweet."

"Thanks." I sneak another glance at the Dancing Queen. When he spins around, I see his little tight ass in those bright pants that might as well be painted on him with blue and white inks. His skinny jeans rival Trent's. To be fair, he doesn't have that bad an ass. I'd grab a handful of it if he wasn't shaking the thing so desperately on that dance floor.

My attention is drawn back to my date when I feel her foot graze my leg. I turn and lift a brow, as if to ask the precise question of: what the fuck? She smiles coyly, as if she's up to nothing, then says, "If you're not into something serious, we can just ... have a little fun back at my place, Mr. old-fashioned." She gives a wink, then sucks down some water from the straw, as if to suggest precisely what sort of "fun" she has in mind.

I'm not gonna lie—I'm tempted. After my recent frequently-recurring dreams involving Trent almost fucking me, I'm charged up as a lightning bolt and ready to be set off by just about anything.

I look back and find the homo's mercifully removed his party-of-one off the dance floor, having taken a seat at the bar. The stool to either side of him once occupied a dude; now they're both empty. He certainly knows how to clear a bar. That's a skill I might like to utilize sometimes on a busy Saturday night.

"What the fuck?"

I return my gaze to Sandy, the source of the outburst. "Huh?"

"You gonna just ignore me all night? A sweet ol' gal like me?" She purses her lips, seeming to suck her tongue in annoyance.

The burger stares me in the face like a half-opened mouth drooling ketchup and gooey diced onions. I've decidedly lost my appetite. "I gotta take a piss."

Ignoring her scandalized face, I abandon the table and slump to the bathroom. When the door shuts behind me, all the clatter and twang of country music and drunken banter goes away. All I'm left with is a wet countertop, two dirty urinals, a stall I couldn't be dared to touch, and a big smudgy mirror through which I see the semi-handsome face of a guy with everything going for him—a guy who will, despite his appeal, be heading home alone tonight. Again.

The door opens behind me and I can't be bothered to turn around, opting to just stare at my own baby blues in the mirror. I think about Trent, wondering what he's doing right now. Is he scaling his girlfriend's wall where some ivy grows? Is he bumping her on her parent's bed? Is he helping her with her math homework?

"You aren't gettin' any prettier."

I turn to look at the bathroom's newest occupant. It's the guy from the dance floor. Upon closer inspection, the angel on his shirt is actually a winged skeleton creature with a sword in either hand. No idea what the fuck it is, but it doesn't look like it takes it up the ass.

"Huh?" I finally respond, still staring at his shirt, studying it.

"Looking at your face in the mirror, you

aren't getting any prettier," he says, coming up to my side to get a look at his own. He presses a few fingers into his cheek, lifting the skin, then letting go and watching it drop. "And neither the fuck am I."

His name's Charlie. We went to school together too, same school Trent and I and every other loser in this town went to, except back then Charlie wasn't so ... colorful. He was just another face in the school band.

He twists his eyes, looking at me from the side of his face. "You gonna hide in here from your date all night? Pretty sure she'd go for you. You're the prettiest guy I see around."

"Don't call me pretty."

"You were missed when you ran off to college for those one and a half tiny years," he goes on as if he didn't hear me. "You, Trent and whoever else thought they could climb outta this hellhole. Welcome back to hell." He gives himself an air-kiss in the mirror.

"What do you mean I was missed?"

"Here, you notice every tiny change. Also

all the hundreds of things that never change. Loneliness is real, girl, and it sucks hard. And not in the below-the-waist way." He squints at me. "Are you really happy here?"

"Yeah," I answer a bit quickly, not really giving it an honest consideration.

He snorts, as if calling me out, then heads to the farthest urinal, unzips his pants. "I'll tell you something," he says as he starts to pee. I look away, rolling my eyes. "It sucks being me in this town. High school was easier when I was pretending to be someone else."

"What the fuck makes you think I care?"

"No one does," he says, finishing and zipping up. The already stuffy room fills with the uproar of a flush. He pushes up next to me to wash his hands. I back out of the way, but only an inch or two. "You pretty boys think you have it all, with your pretty girl dates and your pretty wives and your gym memberships. And really,"—he shuts off the faucet, wipes his hands on his thighs—"you kinda do."

With that, he leaves the bathroom.

It takes me a full minute to gather my resolve and get the hell out of the bathroom. The noise of chatter and thumping country music assaults me, and when I reach my table, the bitch is gone. She left a note on top of my half-eaten burger, scribbled across a napkin: *Thanks for a great time, asshole.* I'm also pretty sure she spit in my drink.

Great. Stranded at my favorite bar in the world, no ride, no date, no nothing. I pull out a twenty, bothered to all hell, and fling it on the table. With one last smirk at the empty dance floor and the idiots guffawing at the bar, I make my leave of Kegs.

Outside in the nearly pitch-dark lot, I pull out my phone and call Trent. Goes straight to voicemail. I call him again, sighing. Again, no answer from fuckface. I imagine him doing things to that probably-underage wonder girl ... things I wish he'd do to me. It pisses me off so much, thinking about the simple things I long for—a cuddle, a kiss, holding hands, being told something nice—and the things I get instead: ditched by my date, sassed by the town homo in the bathroom, and then getting stranded. I could go for an all-nighter with Trent on the X-Box right about now.

I'm about to call him again when I hear the scuffling of shoes against pavement. I turn to see shadows dancing around the bend of the building, somewhere near the dumpsters. At once I assume some sort of mugging or raping or crime is happening and, to my shame, my first instinct is to run away or leap back into the building. For some insane reason, I pursue the noise, coming around the corner.

It's Charlie, pinned against the wall by two flannel-wearing men in cowboy hats. One of them is threatening Charlie verbally, the other one scowling and looking mighty red-faced, even in the dark. What's interesting is the expression on Charlie's face. For being accosted—or robbed or beat up or whatever—by these two considerably larger men, Charlie looks almost ... bored.

"What's going on?" I say loudly.

Only the two men turn their heads to look at me. I recognize one of them: Steve's his name, a jock I knew back in high school. He had an infestation of crabs and had to miss two days of school. He had the "flu", he kept insisting; his ex let everyone know otherwise. "Go away, Benny," he barks, annoyed. "I'm taking care of business."

"What kinda business?" I throw back.

"Taking out the trash," the angry one says to Charlie's face, then spits in it.

Charlie, as unbothered as a snail on the wall, simply smirks and closes one eye, the saliva crawling down his cheek.

Seeing as they're doing this barehanded and without weaponry involved, I dare to take a few steps toward them.

"For two grown men, you sure are taking your time," I remark.

Shouldn't have said that. Incensed by my quip, he throws a fist into Charlie's belly. Charlie rasps, his eyes going wide. Then Steve throws another right into his abdomen, folding

Charlie in half.

I come up next to them. "Go home, dude. You're drunk. I'll finish off the fag."

"When the fuck am I *not* drunk?" Steve snorts at me, then massages his knuckles as if the punch hurt his hand more than Charlie. "This fucker tried to grab my buddy's junk at the bar."

"Yeah," I say, watching as Charlie rises back up, that same bored expression taking his face as he stares at Steve, daring him. "He was checking me out in the bathroom too. Let me take care of him."

Steve, the red rage burning in his eyes, finally backs off, stepping away. His buddy seems to have lost all interest, slumping off toward the parking lot.

When Steve looks at me, he says, "Give him hell. Let him know his kind ain't welcome here. Boy gotta learn to respect, know what I mean? Fuckin' queers think they can touch anything they want."

"I got this."

"Nah. Fuck him up. I wanna watch."

"You're still on probation, aren't you? For that bar fight last month? You don't wanna get caught up in this." I stare at Steve, hard. "Like I said, I *got* this. Go."

Steve snorts, curling and uncurling his fingers several times before finally leaving. I stand in front of Charlie now, my bright eyes locked onto his dark, daring ones. I listen as the two cowboys walk away. I hear the roar of a truck like some mighty dragon in the dark, and then it slithers away into the night.

When there is only silence, in a quiet, calm voice, I say, "What the heck were you doing grabbin' some guy's junk, Charlie?"

"I didn't grab nothin'," he says tiredly with half-open eyelids. "Only thing I'm guilty of is being a queer. Oops, sue me." He smirks and looks away, tired of it all.

I don't really believe him, to be honest. I'm pretty sure he did something at the bar, considering how forward he was with me in the damn bathroom. Pretty boy this, pretty boy that. Part of me wants to say he asked for this, what with the way he was acting.

I'm not sure what the other part of me feels. "You alright otherwise?"

"Dandy."

I look him over. "You ... got a car?"

He looks at me, suspicious. "Yes. Why? You gonna try and take it from me?"

"No. I need a ride home."

"And ... that's my problem, how?"

"I just saved you from getting your ass kicked," I retort, feeling my breath go all over his face. He blinks it away. "You owe me."

"I got gut-punched. Twice. I could've handled them myself. I owe you nothin' but a swift kick in the balls," he says, then looks down my body, reconsidering. "Or a swift lick *of* your balls, whichever you'd allow."

I feel my cock jump in my pants, hearing that. "Neither."

"I could'a taken them both," he insists again. "Steve and his wannabe cowboy."

"In the ass?"

He smiles suddenly, impressed by my wit, I guess. Then, looking smart, he says, "I'll give you that ride. And I promise to keep my hands to myself, so long as you let me blast whatever I want on the radio."

Car ride of gay hell, party of two. "Deal."

[4]

When we pull up to the apartment, I have to listen to Charlie complaining about a cramp in his stomach. I tell him to sleep it off but he insists on *drinking* it off, as I made the mistake of telling him that I didn't like my roommate's choice of beer—which happens to be Charlie's favorite too, apparently. "Please," he begs me, then fakes a pain in his belly. "Ugh. Please. I need some healing. The beer's gonna do my body *and* my mind good, please, please."

I might have more than one reason for saying yes. And I do.

When the door shuts behind him, he seems to forget all about the beer and walks around my place, looking at everything. It bothers me, the way he *looks* at everything. "Is this you?" he asks stupidly, picking up a framed graduation photo.

"No, that's my gay twin." I swing open the fridge, poking around leftover Chinese and half-empty sauce bottles looking for the beer.

"Well, your gay twin is hot." He sets the picture back down, keeps drifting around the room. "Where's your roomie?"

"He's busy statutorily raping a girl for the weekend." I'd finally gotten ahold of Trent on the car ride here. He wanted to hear all about the date I had. Then, after I told him, he wanted to know why I was such a prick to such a perfectly nice girl like ... what's-her-name. I ignored the lecture and told him he could stay there for the weekend; I wouldn't be needing the car. To say he sounded relieved is an understatement.

Maybe I should've lied and said I needed

the car. Thinking about what he's doing to that girl—things he should be doing to me—makes my face red and my cock stir.

An hour later, the TV hums with the applause of a game show, the air conditioning unit grumbles tiredly at the window, and I'm doing the last thing on Earth I'd expect to be doing: throwing back beers with Charlie.

"Oooh my," he sings after guffawing at something I said about a girl we both knew in high school. "That bitch *crazy*, tellin' ya. Did I mention she tried to sell me *popsicles?*"

"No. Hmm, I like popsicles."

"So do I," he says, his eyes going big. "I'm pretty sure it was on a grape creamsicle that I learned how to suck my first cock."

I laugh hard. Too hard. For some reason, I sorta want him to think I'm drunker than I really am. The couch can sit about four people, yet Charlie and I are puddled in the middle of it, much in the same way Trent and I usually sit. It's a mind-fuck, really, that tonight I'm sitting by someone I *could* make a move on.

But for all my bravery, I'm just not *that* brave. "This is why no one talks to you," I say after I'm done laughing, hoping my words sound naturally slurred. I've kicked back three beers; I need at least eight more in me before I'm *actually* drunk. "All you talk about is sex. You're gross, Charlie."

"And you 'straight' boys don't talk about sex and pussy and how many ways you can bend a girl over a table? Puh-*leeze*." He grabs another can, cracks it open, chugs, then says, "I'm downright *tame* compared to you horn dogs. What the hell am I guilty of? Dancing too much at the bar? I got life in me. This is my life. Fuck you for making me feel like I shouldn't live it." He chugs the rest, crushes the can in his fist, throws it over the back of the couch. "I should warn you, with regard to the amount of alcohol I've consumed tonight, I had a head start at the bar." He hiccups.

I've been nursing the same can for the last thirty minutes. I don't think he's noticed. "It isn't easy to just ... be yourself in this town."

"It isn't *possible*," says Charlie, like he's correcting me. "You grow up being told what you gotta be by your parents, because they can't just let you be what you are. Then you're made fun of, beat up, shoved around by your peers in school. Then you meet some jackasses in high school who tell you who you are, then also proceed to beat you up for it, emotionally or physically, both count as bad. I should warn you I'm drunk."

"You already did. But I never perceived you as a guy who ... *isn't* himself. You've always just been ..." I try to think of a nice way to say it.

"The town fag, yeah, whatever. You think that's not a role in itself? Half the time, *I* don't even feel like I'm me. Are *you* ever really you, Benny? Even around your roommate? Or your buddies, or ... or that sweet girl you totally failed to woo at Kegs?" His eyes go wide and his face takes a sudden yellowish color.

"Don't vomit on my couch," I request of him as politely as I can.

"Puh-leeze," he manages to say, cocking his neck. "I'm a tank. I can rest the down of these. I can—I can down the rest of ... What the fuck did I just say?"

Then he leans into me, his cheek pressed against my shoulder. I'm suddenly very aware of how fast my heart is beating. I feel the weight of his face on my shoulder, pressing into my side. I've never done anything with a guy before. I've never had a guy—especially a gay guy—this close to me, this close to *doing* something to me. All these years I've been waiting by Trent's side like a sad puppy ... and I might get my first break from Charlie. Is this really happening?

He burps, then wipes his mouth and sits back up. "Sorry," he says, though I totally don't want to accept his apology for anything. "Sorry. I'm clearly as think as I drunk I am, know what I'm sayin'? Heh, heh." He reels his head, sighing.

Lean into me again. Please. Please lean into me. "You can crash here if you want."

"Mmm," he moans, seeming to consider. That is, if he heard me at all. He leans back into the cushions, shutting his eyes. The TV drones on and on, I'm not even paying attention.

At the beginning of the night, I was more annoyed about Charlie's existence than I was about my forced date. Now, Charlie is suddenly the indubitable center of my focus and desires, the only person in the world who can supply what I'm demanding, the source of all my hidden thrills and secret needs and pent-up cravings, years-long in the making.

I shift my weight on the couch, then allow my shoulder to press into his when I lean back. As if by instinct, I spread my legs a bit, the crotch of my jeans out in the open. I'm hard, I know it, just with the anxious thought, with the excitement, with the anticipation, the *possibility* that I could be touched by another guy. I let the can rest in my hand on one side of my body, and let my other hand rest on my belly, out of the way.

Nothing there to stop Charlie from having his way with me.

After what seems like an eternity, he moans again, as if trying to form a word. Then I hear his head shift, as if he's looking, as if he's noticed what I put out in front of him, the temptation.

Please be tempted. I lick my lips too, just in case he's looking at my face.

"I'm really drunk," he murmurs, slurring. His voice is *so* close to my ear that I feel chills run down my body, goose bumps brought to life along my arms. He whispers something else that I can't distinguish, and then he shifts his weight.

His hand drops onto my thigh.

I resist the gasp that tries to come out of my mouth. My heart is hammering so loudly it's a wonder he can't hear it ... it's a wonder it isn't shaking the floorboards loose beneath my feet. I have never wanted something so badly. It isn't even Trent. He's not even Trent and yet my entire body is squirming beneath the skin, craving another man's touch, craving the attention, craving the closeness.

Touch me, I'm begging him. *Move your hand. Touch me.*

His hand begins to slide. Slowly. Slowly. Glacially. It might take him an hour to make it from my thigh to my crotch. *I will wait that entire hour, holding my breath.* I don't move an inch of my body. Not one muscle flinches, not even my bone-hard cock. It's like a hunt, and any sudden movements can scare away my prey. Touch me. Grope me. Be inappropriate. Don't be noble. Don't be careful. Touch me.

Touch me.

He keeps sliding his hand. He reaches my inner thigh. I fight an urge to squirm. I fight another urge to moan. I struggle with all my might not to twitch or feel ticklish.

I wore my tight jeans today. Every graze of his fingertips is like touching my skin. I might as well be naked, thighs spread, with the misbehaving hand of Charlie tracing my leg and sliding ever-slowly between them.

Touch me.

Grope me.

His weight on the couch shifts more and I feel his shoulder digging into mine. Then, to my surprise, I feel his mouth on my chest. *His mouth.* The button-down blue plaid shirt I'm wearing clings to my skin, and when he puts his mouth on my pec, I feel his warm touch as though he were using tongue.

His lips move. My toes curl.

I'm so hard I'm leaking.

He moves his mouth again. I feel his chin graze my nipple. Is it safe yet to let out the gasp I'm swallowing? Is it safe to acknowledge what he's doing to me?

His hand, which had stopped moving on my thigh, begins once again to slide, almost startling me. It draws closer to my crotch, up my inner thigh, drawing closer and closer while his mouth works on my chest, suckling my pec.

Charlie gets bolder. He brings his other hand to my chest and, slowly, carefully as if trying not to wake me, he undoes the top button of my shirt. *Oh god.* I feel the tightness of my shirt let go, just with that one button. He runs his wicked fingers down, releases the next button. The tightness drops again, my pecs closer to falling out. *Oh god, it's happening.* My heart is pounding. My whole body is quaking, aching, and ready.

He moves his hand yet again, works off the next button, and my chest spills out. *Fuck, fuck, fuck.* His warm breath brushes across my pec, across my nipple, and I release the subtlest of sighs—I can't help it. I'm suddenly not so sure I *want* to help it.

Maybe I should tell him ... but what would I say? I crave my roommate? I'm only doing this with you because I can't have who I really want? I'm straight by all definitions of lifestyle, yet hungry for a specific kind of intimacy that only another man can give?

When his mouth suckles my nipple, all my thoughts are lost, and I drop open my mouth, overcome. His tongue works my nipple so expertly that it feels like a blow job. It might as well be, for all the mind-blowing effect it's having on my cock, which throbs and leaks in my tight jeans.

As if responding to said tightness, his hand moves again. This time, it reaches its long-awaited destination, the fingers running slowly across the bulge my cock is making in my jeans. *Oh god. Fuck, fuck, fuck.* It's like he knows exactly where my cock is without even looking, as his face is pressed into my pec, his mouth latched to my nipple like a suction cup, and his tongue *just won't stop.* His hand expertly traces my cock through the jeans, up one side, down the other, up one side, down the other.

It's driving me insane.

Then the activity at my nipple stops. He lifts off my chest, then withdraws his hand. It is so abrupt, I flick open my eyes and turn to him, startled. He's looking at me with a strange mixture of guilt and excitement in his eyes. What happened?

"Sorry," he slurs, hiccups, then repeats, "so sorry, Benny. I didn't mean to—"

"Huh?" I say, stupid as ever, unwilling to acknowledge what he was doing to me, even now, even in my current state.

"I'm drunk. You're drunk. We're such a mess, the b-b-both of us." He burps just then, guttural and bassy. Then he wipes his mouth and, after a moment of thought, adds, "I don't want to take advantage of you, Benny. You're a good guy. I could've beat those fuckers up myself, but you came and acted like some knight in shining armor and like ... I'm a big sucker for the knight in shining armor, okay? And I'm lonely. And you're here. And—" He loses his words, staring at me expectantly.

Why can't I just say it? Why can't I tell him to keep doing what he's doing? He's waiting for permission. He wants permission. Here I am, a block of muscle and fear, a big tangle of hunger and needs. Didn't he just feel my boner? Doesn't he get that I want it, too?

Why do I have to say it?

"You're a good guy, Benny." He reaches up, which excites me for a second, until I realize he's doing my shirt buttons back up. One, then two, then the top button.

My cock is throbbing. My insides, whimpering.

"W-What're you doing?" I finally get out, sounding as stupid as I feel. "W-What do you mean?"

"I've overstepped a bit. I took advantage of you."

He puts a hand on my shoulder, patting me, then thinks the better of it and just gets up from the couch.

No, no, no, no, no.

"Wait," I blurt out, getting up, watching him as he walks to the door. "Wait, Charlie. I told you, man, you can crash here. I trust you. We're cool, right?"

He stops at the door, looks at me hard, his hungry eyes drawing a path from my crotch to my face. Then he says, "To be honest, I don't trust myself."

After he leaves, the only sound I'm left with is the pounding of a heart against my ribcage like some sickly, starved prisoner begging for release.

[5]

Trent doesn't return from his weekend with his high school prom queen until about midafternoon Monday, just before I'm heading in for work. He looks like a number's been done on him. I likely look the same, with all his beer I've been guzzling. Hope he doesn't mind. I'll consider it a price for not having a car all weekend due to his teenager-lust. In fact, I was about to *walk* the thirty minutes down the street to work before he showed up.

"Need the keys," I say as he drops into the couch right where Charlie was two nights ago.

"I almost encountered the dad." Trent sighs, wipes his face and turns to look at me. "You totally fuck things up with Sandy, or did she forgive you and you fucked her brains out last night?"

This one time back in eighth grade, we went to a party where they played a weird combination of spin-the-bottle and seven-minutes-in-heaven. There were approximately four other boys there, all four of which I would've given *anything* to be stuck in a closet with. I didn't even know what I'd do with them. I just wanted to be near them, for them to like me. I'd never been kissed, but I was sure I'd like it to be one of them. When I spun the blue hairbrush, which we were using as our bottle, it landed between the adorable punk boy Trent Hollings ... and goth Katy Windsor. Boy and girl. Of course, as the way of assumptions go, that meant my "bottle" had chosen Katy. My heart sank as Katy got up and took me to the closet, the hooting and howling of the others meant to encourage us.

Once in the dark, though, she slumped against the wall and sighed. Through the cracks in the slatted door, I could see her face. *What's wrong?* I asked her. She told me she really wanted her first kiss to be with Trent, and that's why she sat by him. I had to smile because I was thinking the same thing. How nice it would've been if the group had laughed, played along with the hairbrush and decided that I had to go into the closet with Trent. My heart leapt at the thought. I told Katy it was okay, that she could save her first kiss for a boy she really wanted to kiss. She looked a touch grateful and a touch sad. Then, for the next six and a half minutes, we didn't touch at all, sitting alone together in the darkness and listening to each other breathe.

"I fucked my right hand last night," I answer the now-ten-years-older Trent. "But thanks for asking, buddy. I was about to walk to work, but now that you're here and I got the car back, I have about twenty minutes before I gotta leave. Wanna play Wii? Some Smash?"

"You're gonna need to walk, actually." Trent kicks his feet up—two oversized chucks with the laces half-undone—and throws his arms over the back of the couch. He's wearing a black leather cuff on his right wrist that I'd gotten him last year for his birthday. "I have a job interview at five."

I come up to the back of the couch. "What happened to your other job?"

"I think my boss is into me. Like, *into me.* That's gross and it makes me uncomfortable, so I put in applications elsewhere."

His boss is a blond-haired man in his forties whose name is Donald, but he goes by Dick. "So, you're scared of Dick. That's what you're telling me. You're letting Dick scare you away."

"When Dick's trying to touch *my* dick, yeah." He turns on the TV, tosses the remote on the cushion next to him.

"Never know. You might like it."

"*You* might like it," he jests back. If only he knew. But he doesn't, and never will.

"You talk about *me* flakin' out on dates," I point out, "and here you are, flakin' out on a job because you can't stand someone checking you out who isn't a girl."

"Whatever, it's gross." He changes the channel, plops the remote back down.

Even after knowing each other so long and having spent years talking about our private lives and wants and fears, I still don't know if he *really* knows about me. So every time he says something about gay men being gross, I can't tell if he *intends* to hurt me, or if it's pure ignorance and he might not say those things if he knew. Thinking this, guilt rushes in, and I'm staring at the back of Trent's head, his spiky black punk hair, and my stomach's roiling.

Am I in the wrong for keeping this secret from him for so long? Am I a terrible friend, to keep this huge part of me hidden from Trent ...?

I imagine how that other night might've been, had Trent been the one passed out on my couch, and I was the one latched to his nipple, running my hand up his inner thigh, waking parts of him he didn't know were asleep.

Staring at the keys he left on the counter, I sigh, resigning myself to the thirty minute walk in this unforgiving summer heat. I have half a mind to grab the keys and drive myself anyway, forcing him to get a ride or walk to his own interview, but as usual, I allow Trent to have whatever he wants, take whatever he wants, get whatever he wants, no matter how much I suffer for it.

I spoil him. I kinda want to spoil him.

"Will you pick me up after work?" I ask. "I get off at ten. I really hate to walk home in the dark."

"Nah. I'll be at Kirkland's. He's havin' one of his beer fests tonight, remember? Marked it on the Star Trek."

I give a tired glance at the Star Trek calendar he's referring to. He and I jokingly told his mom that we are huge Trekkies, and every year since then, she gets us a Star Trek calendar. I doubt either of us have seen a single episode or movie.

"That's tonight?" I bite my lip. "But—"

"It's just three blocks north from your work, ain't it? Maybe four, five. Come by after you get off. It goes 'til, like, whenever A.M. His house is huge. There'll be pussy aplenty. And probably high schoolers, if that's your thing. Just kidding. Not really kidding. Loud music. Lots of dancing and probably weed, if we're lucky." He pushes himself off the couch, comes around the counter to the kitchen.

Watching his ass in those skinny jeans of his, ruefully I say, "We're never lucky. Not in this fuck-all of a town." Then, I grab my wallet, shove my phone into a pocket and head for the door.

"Hey, where's all my beer?" I hear him ask as I shut the door behind me.

[6]

The scent of smoke, sweat, and barbeque precedes the party by about three blocks. I admit, my shift at work was not that long tonight, but here I am slumping down a dark street to Kirkland's fat pad of sin. And I'm still in my work uniform, which consists of khakis, brown belt, loafers and a white chest-hugging polo with nametag. I couldn't look dorkier if I tried. Even my hair's parted because, well, I can't stand to make a bad impression, even at my day job of the past however-many-years.

I find Trent on the porch with Steve.

"Hey, fuckface," says Trent, raising the bottle he's drinking as if in a toast. "You're finally here, I see. Why so late?"

"Had to close because Pete didn't show up, otherwise I would've been here an hour ago." I squint through the window where likely everyone under the age of twenty-five in this godforsaken town has gathered. And maybe a few much younger, too. "Why does it smell like horse poop?"

"We drank up all the soda and the punch that Emma brought over," Trent goes on while Steve just stares at me with red, drunken eyes, "but there's Miller in the mini-fridge."

I nod at the pair of them. "Appreciated. I'll be back."

I need to be drunk if I want to get through this. Like, super drunk. Like, fall on my face, fuck-off, lips-against-the-floorboards drunk.

Inside, the house looks like the electric bill wasn't paid. A dark entryway (with a couple making out by the stairs) spills into a den area where about seven people are all over the couch, illuminated by the glow of a TV. I can't and don't want to be able to see what they're doing to each other, judging from the wet sounds I hear. Further in the house, the larger living room is flooded with dancing fools, and the farthest wall overlooks a backyard through tall floor-to-ceiling windows.

"Where the fuck's the kitchen?" I mutter to myself, pushing through the crowd of half-standing, half-gyrating bodies toward an archway that I pray leads me into the kitchen. Instead, it leads me to the dining room where two girls are seated at the table, chatting.

When one of them catches my eye, my stomach drops. "Hi," I say to Sandy, my date from the other night.

"Hello, Benny." She regards me coolly, her lips squeezed into a permanent smirk. Her friend, a girl with a sideways ponytail, simply watches me as though I were the menacing dog who happened on a pair of kittens.

"Having a—a—a good time?" I finally get out, inching my way through the room.

"Marginally," answers Sandy. The friend remains silent as a crypt.

"Great." I force myself to smile at them both. My transparent, cheesy politeness goes unreturned. "I didn't have a chance to change after work, otherwise I'd—"

"You look fine." The friend interrupts, lifting her brows at me. Sandy gives her a quick, disapproving nudge with her elbow. The friend, after a glance at Sandy, clears her throat and draws silent.

I nod at them. "Gonna grab myself a beer. I'll see you two later."

Knowing full well that at least one of them has no desire to see me later, I say it anyway, then move into the kitchen.

Pressed into the counter by the sink are three guys in jeans. One of them's shirtless, sporting a distractingly nice set of abs, and the other two wear t-shirts. The tall one to the left has a cowboy hat on and a beer in his hairy fist. He's first to look at me, but doesn't greet me in any way except for a suspicious squint.

The other two are occupied in conversation ... or maybe it's more of an argument about something to do with barbells.

"Excuse me," I say as I draw near the tall one who's leaning on the fridge. He shifts his weight to the counter next to him as I pull open the door. Nothing but cheese and a gallon of milk and a bin of potatoes meets my eyes. I frown.

"Mini-fridge's upstairs," says the tall one, "if you're looking for the good stuff."

"At this point I'm looking for *any* stuff." I meet his eyes, shutting the fridge. I extend a hand. "I'm Benny."

"I know. We went to school together, just never talked is all. You got—?" Then, he cuts himself off, distracted by a girl passing through the kitchen. She gives him a onceover, smiles, then disappears into the doorway connecting back into the den with the TV. "You got ... Sorry, forgot my dang question. That lady was *fine*."

Straight guys and their dicks. "No prob."

"Dude, there's so many fine chicks here," one of the other guys—the shirtless one—says. "Never even seen half of them before. Tony, if we don't get laid tonight—"

"Good point," the tall one I was talking to, Tony, says, then excuses himself wordlessly from the kitchen in pursuit of the girl.

The two at the sink watch him go off, then drop back into their conversation as if I'm not even here. What I wouldn't give to draw as much of their attention as the pretty girls do. What I wouldn't give to not be so pathetically dependent on Trent's approving glances and smiles and laughter ... to have any hot guy of my choice at this party, the shirted *and* the shirtless ones. I give another doleful onceover of the young dude's abs, feeling a pang of desire stir my heart. He doesn't notice my ogling, which is both fortunate and unfortunate. No hot dude ever seems to notice me, not in the way I want to be noticed.

Pity party for one. I abandon the kitchen, pass through the den of eerily quiet souls and ascend the stairs to the second floor. Leaning over the banister is another pair of guys staring down at the selection of girls dancing in the living room. One of them comments about a pretty one in a pink dress, to which the other makes an obscene show of humping the banister, I guess to portray to his buddy what exactly he plans to do with her, despite it looking like he's ramming some dude in the ass. Or maybe it's just my oversexed mind.

The game room on the second floor has a pool table that is being used for anything but a proper game. Bottles and cans line its perimeter, and a pair of guys that can't be older than sixteen or so are seated atop it, talking to one another and stealing glances at the other young girls across the room who are laughing about something.

Boys with girls. Girls with boys. This is all my life is full of in this fucking town. When I was in high school suffering the same fate, school dance after school dance after school dance, I was convinced that my life would change when I graduated. I dreamed a hundred dreams of what my college experience would be like, about the freedom I'd exercise, about the boys I'd meet and the love I'd find. Instead, I took Trent with me, and he was the dangerous light bulb toward which my stupid moth self was inevitably lured. I spent those almost-two college years being boy-blind, then dropped out with him and returned home with nothing to show but a list of half a hundred things I swore I'd do when I left ... and didn't.

Ah, there it is. "Pardon me, ladies." I make for the mini-fridge near them. They draw quiet and seem to just watch me as I feel around for a bottle, then pull it out and snap off the top. "Thanks." I give them a smile, then take a swig. Reconsidering, I grab another bottle for later, then dismiss myself from the game room to let the boys resume their dumb fascination with the two pretty girls they're obviously too chicken shit to approach. *Just fuck each other already*, I have more than half a mind to shout.

The same two guys are at the banister still, staring down at the crowd of dancers. So many people from town are here, I wonder if Charlie is among them. With Steve poised on the porch like some ugly watchdog, I doubt he'd let Charlie through the doors. The thought angers me, even if I'm not super attracted to Charlie or excited about his presence. For some reason, the fact that Charlie even exists in a town like this gives me a bizarre, unknowing strength. It makes me feel like I'm not alone, even if Charlie and I are so ... unalike. We at least have that *one thing* in common, even if Charlie himself isn't aware. Thinking of him makes me feel the gentle touch of a hand on my inner thigh and, frustratingly, I feel my cock stir. *Not now, dummy.*

I take another swig from the bottle. Fuck it all. I'm so alone.

The music has grown louder somehow, and when I poke a finger through the blinds in the front entryway, I notice Trent's missing and only Steve sits out there now, staring out at the nothingness in the street. His brown-booted foot is propped up on the porch railing and a cigarette dangles from his left hand. I sneer at him through the window, then release the blinds and walk away, wondering where Trent's gone.

Just as always, I'm puppy-dogging the focal point of my existence, my rope and tether, my black hole of a crush that is ruefully named Trent. *Where the fuck did he go?* He's not in the den with the creepy TV-watchers and whatever-else-have-you's. Unless he slipped into a bedroom, he's not upstairs. I doubt he's in the kitchen because there's no beverages left there.

I move through the living room, deciding to give the backyard a combing-over. The guys, who don't look old enough to be drinking, are generally at one end of the living room, chatting, joking, some of them dancing stupidly, but most of their eyes are shooting arrows of desire at the spread of girls across the room, hoping any of their arrows stick. Regular cupids, all of those dumb fucks. The girls are just as stupid, doing the same thing. They sip their drinks, shake their bodies to the music, laughing at one another's jokes while they shoot quick glances at the guys. Is this a fucking school dance? It's just the forever, inevitable mating ritual dance bullshit of heterokind. Much like the inevitable mating ritual dance bullshit of homokind, except I'm likely the only fucking gay guy here. None of those guys shoot longing glances my way.

I squeeze shut my eyes, frustrated, and finish off the bottle, abandoning it atop an end table by the couch before pushing out the back door. A barbeque pit still smokes where, likely a few hours ago, some actually edible food was being grilled. I still haven't seen Kirkland, and with his bushy head of hair and pointy beard, he's impossible to miss. There aren't many people out here, but with it being so dark, I can't quite make out who's sitting in lawn chairs by the inflated baby pool.

Then, Trent emerges from the dark like a ghost. "Where ya been?"

"Got lost in the house looking for booze." I lift my second bottle I haven't cracked open yet to indicate. "Where the fuck's Kirk?"

"When's our lease up, bud?" he asks quietly, drawing himself up to my side. "Do you know?"

I frown. "What do you mean?"

"The lease. My mom wanted to know." He chugs from his can. It crinkles loudly in his squeezing fist, dripping with condensation onto his shirt.

"Why do you—Why does she ... need to know that?" I feel my heart racing and not in the good way.

"Never mind." He belches, not meeting my eyes and, instead, peering through the window back into the house. "Fuckin' full of nobodies. Who the hell did Kirkland invite, the fuckin' high school? Where's the assholes *our* age? Hope the walk wasn't that bad, bud. Girls here aren't even that hot."

I'm still lost figuring out his question. Is he thinking of moving out? "Are we alright?"

He frowns, annoyed. "Of course we're alright. What the fuck." He chugs again.

I know Trent. He's never evasive about anything. He's blunt with me, always is. His hesitation and his weirdness unsettles me like nothing else in this stinking town can. I'm flooded with a million guilty thoughts all at once. Does he know? Did he figure it out? Did Charlie fucking say something? Did he find something on my computer? For that matter, what the fuck *is* on my computer?

But I can't say any of this. I can't even express it in some vague, indirect way. I'm stuck with my worries while Trent guzzles his beers, checks out his ladies, and goes about his life with no regard or awareness whatsoever to the war being waged in my mind. The same war I've been fighting since we were dumb horny teens and jerked off while staring at differently stimulating ... things.

We were fourteen when I first stayed

overnight at his house. He wanted to show me something and it wasn't until 2 AM when he had the porn open on his computer that I realized what. I'll never forget those fake perky tits and the grunts she made as the frat boys fucked her one by one. I never really got to see the frat boys very well, as this was straight porn—I think—but it didn't matter when I had Trent pulling out his wiener right next to me, going to town. Some wicked part of my mind wanted to feign "not knowing what to do" around him. My heart raced, almost to the point of nausea, almost to the point of throwing up his mom's brownies she made us earlier. I wanted him to touch me so bad. He got hard to the porn. I got hard to him, watching him breathe heavy, watching him gnaw on his own lip, watching his face wrinkle up as he grew closer and closer and closer to the edge.

When he came, a string of his cum landed on my face. I shut my eyes and gasped, feeling it run across my tongue and lips.

He laughed and laughed and laughed.

And then I came, too.

"You see Sandy inside?" he asks, slapping my belly and jerking me out of the memory. "She was upstairs, last I saw."

"She's in the dining room," I say flatly. "She saw me. Can't say she liked it."

He throws an arm over my shoulder suddenly, as if sensing my withdrawal, and pulls me into him. "Patch things up, dude. She's forgiving. You two could really hit it off. You could finally have a girl in your life."

"What if I don't want a girl in my life?"

The thought came so suddenly that I voiced it without thinking twice. A rush of dread reddens my face. Trent's lips are near my nose, his alcohol breath wafting over me as he breathes.

"What else you gonna have in your life?" he asks innocently, missing the point I might have been making.

You, Trent. You, you, you. You are all I want. You are all I need. You and your breath and your slender punk body and your cocky charm. You and your competitiveness. You and your annoying habits I can't stand. You and the way you've made me feel around you for over a decade. You are everything to me.

But there will come a time when he meets a girl, and that girl actually sticks. She won't be a prom queen nominee from the high school around whose parents he has to tiptoe. It won't be any of the easy girls at the bar, none of whom he actually picks up, despite throwing each and every one of them at me, Sandy included. But he will meet a girl and she will be everything he dreamed of. And I will have to be invited to the wedding. I'll be the best man, standing at his side, watching him be taken away by another girl I'll be forced to like. Hell, maybe I'll even *actually* like her. Wouldn't that be worse? I'll have no reason under the stars to protest their marriage, no reason to talk him out of it. She'll be perfect and sweet and friendly and beautiful. She'll even be pro-gay or some shit.

And I'll still hate her. I'll hate her for taking him from me. I'll hate her and I'll hate him. And for all the rest of my days, I'll live under the shadow of some fantasy I should've thrown away the year I grew my first pube.

"Probably just more beer," I answer him finally, wondering how true my answer, in fact, really is. I stare at my half-empty bottle, lost in thoughts of a future without him. I'd never even considered one, but I'm no longer a kid. I'm an adult. I'm an adult who's running out of time.

What am I doing?

Trent slaps his neck suddenly, curses. "I'm heading back inside. Getting bit the fuck up out here. You comin'?"

Aren't I always? I nod.

We move into the living room again. The boys on one side, the girls on the other, and a sea of reluctance between them. Kicking back my new bottle, I laugh on the inside at the dumbness of the scenario in front of me. All these horned up, lonely, desperate folk of my horned up, desperate town ... and they can't even approach each other at a party. What is this, high school? People are already coupled off in bedrooms and dens and backyards and wherever else, yet the pump of dance music paralyzes these fools.

"Feel like headin' home yet?" asks Trent. "This party's lame."

And full of high schoolers, judging from the fear they have of the opposite sex. Even the twenty-somethings in the crowd won't look at me. None of those hot boys will give me the time of day or night. None of them see me. None of them know. I study the crowd long and hard, feeling brave.

"Actually, I feel like dancing."

Trent looks at me, thinking I'm crazy, when I slap my bottle of beer into his chest and push myself out onto the floor. Two girls look at me, startled by my suddenly popping into existence. They become my inspiration. I start working my shoulders to the music. One of the girls smiles. The song pumps harder, and then my hips start to rock, my arms working into the sexy-bad performance I'm putting on. Now I have four girls looking at me, a small grouping of them, all of their eyes at perfect attention to my seduction act. I grin, emboldened by their excitement, and move my hips harder. I lift my arms in the air.

The girls begin to circle me like a flock of birds, and now their bodies are moving too. The music wraps us up in some sort of trance. What do you know? I'm part of the heterokind mating ritual, my arms twisting, my hips working an invisible hula-hoop, feet stamping the floor. I can't take the smile off my face, all the pretty birds circling me and shaking their feathers and laughing. I'm suddenly the most charming blue jay that's flown into their lady-tree. At long last, after an eternity of waiting here at this party for something to happen, I pull them out of the darkness.

When I turn around, I see the eyes of all eighteen or nineteen boys across the room. All of their eyes, *all of them*, are on me.

They envy me. They want to be me. They want all these women to be all over them.

I am their focal point, in this one moment. I am their everything. I am their cream and their butter and their prize in the cereal box.

All the boys are watching *me* now.

But the reality is, no one's winning. These girls are grinding their hips for me—for a guy who will never choose or prefer any of them. The boys across the room, they're now the ones pining for something they can't have, at least not right now. They're drooling in envy. They're wondering who I am. They're curious and infatuated and dreaming, just like me.

And Trent on the sidelines, watching all this happen. Trent and his punk boy lips and his lip ring. Trent and his messy dark hair, giving him that air of mystery and sexuality and depth. Trent and the utterly bewildered expression on his face ... and my beer bottle that still hangs in his slackening grip.

All of us, playing the lonely game. All of us, losers.

[7]

I can't sleep.

I close my eyes and dream Trent is trying to dance with me, pushing his hips into mine and gripping me the way he grips the girls. *Stop*, I try to tell him, shoving him off, knowing he's fucking with me. He drunk.

Stop.

Then, his mouth lunges for my face. He's trying to kiss me and I shove at him, but can't push him away far enough. *Stop trying to kiss me*, the dream-version of me says while the dream-version of him keeps reaching.

He laughs drunkenly in my face. I even feel the heat of his breath as if it's there. He grips me harder, suddenly having all the power and strength of the world in those hands of his.

He always had that power.

Even in my dreams.

It doesn't matter what I do. I push his shoulders, his mouth seems to grow closer. I push his hips, they grind me harder. Harder. That's the key word: *harder*. My cock grows and grows, and it isn't wholly pleasurable.

I've never hated a boner more than I have tonight. Every tossing and turning in the bed runs my hard-on along the sheets, stimulating it worse, tickling it, sending shivers up my spine that I resent.

Stop doing this to me.

He never stops.

Then, when the struggle is almost too much to bear, I turn and find him just staring at me, almost hurt. He asks me something, his lips moving, and I don't understand. *What?*

He asks again, but I still don't hear him.

Does he really want to kiss me? Have I had it wrong all along?

The rhythm of the music is a heartbeat. The walls bend inward with each beat, synchronized. It scares me. My heart races.

What are you trying to say, Trent?

His mouth grows closer.

Does he really want to kiss me?

When I open my mouth to finally accept his, he shoves a sock in it.

I wake up in the darkness of my room, alone, and Trent isn't there, neither the real one nor the imaginary. I stare down my body, my sheets forming a huge teepee with my boner pointing at the ceiling fan.

"I've had worse dreams," I say out loud, miserably.

Deciding I can't sleep at all, I drag myself out of the room in just boxers and gym shorts and a white tank. The subtle titter of voices on the TV draws my attention, surprising me. *Trent's still awake?* I come to the living room and find Trent leaning back in the middle of the couch, his feet propped up on the coffee table and the remote hanging in his left hand.

He's asleep.

I listen to the calm ins and outs of his breath. His eyes closed, his lips slightly open, he looks so ... adorable. I envy his peace. I can't remember the last time I fell asleep at his side while on the couch.

I miss that so much.

I've wanted nothing but to fall asleep with him, curled up, his arms draped across me carelessly. Maybe when we're asleep, he'll absently put his leg over me, hugging me like a fireman's pole, with his face nuzzled into my neck like a pillow, not even minding that I'm a dude.

Why can't guys be like that? I don't even need him to be gay. I just want him to comfort me. We've been through a lot. We're closer than most brothers who are related by blood.

Why do guys have to be so ... afraid? Why can't they be more ...

All these struggles bring me to the end of the couch. When I get a full look at him, I realize he's only in his boxers. I see the tattoo he got when he turned eighteen, a big scorpion on his shoulder. His boxers are black and hug his thighs—which makes the wood inside them show all the more. I stare at it, surprised. His legs somewhat spread, his arms across the back of the couch, his slender, toned body painted the bluish glow from the TV, I find myself completely entranced.

I'm such a fool. I fall in love every single time I see him. I fall in love over and over.

I lower myself to the arm of the couch, watching Trent, listening to him breathe. My heart is literally jumping out of my chest, yearning for him.

Why do I like him? He's not even always nice. But ... he includes me, most of the time. He's kept gravitating back to me over the years. I've always been there. I'm dependable. Even in college when I was sure he'd make a hundred other friends, he seemed to only bother keeping my company. What if there's something there? What if ...

What if ...

I put my hand on the back of the couch to brace myself, misjudge where it is, and slip off the arm, landing clumsily on the couch, halfway into Trent's lap.

I freeze. I don't move a muscle. I turn to stone.

Trent fidgets, his breath changing for a second, and then he resettles in the same position, his legs outstretched and apart, feet on the coffee table, and his arms still over the back of the couch. He's still asleep.

Still asleep.

And here I am, a hand on each cushion to either side of him, hovered over him with my face an inch from his crotch. His hard cock, tenting his boxers, threatens to poke me in the eye. Ever so fucking slowly, I turn my head, looking up at his face.

His eyes are still closed, his mouth still hanging partway open, and he breathes slowly, in he breathes, a long moment, then out he breathes, a long moment, then in ...

My heart is racing so hard. I feel a certain dark inspiration brewing inside me from my night with Charlie. What he did to me ... the excitement I felt ...

What if Trent has just been ... waiting? What if he's awake right now, pretending to be asleep? What if ...

What if ...

Balancing all my weight on one hand, I lift the other and, so, so, so, *so* gently, I take a pinch of his boxers between my fingers.

I look up to check his eyes. Still closed. Still asleep.

I give my fingers a gentle tug. The fly to his boxers moves a smidge. I give it another tender pull, sliding it. I hear Trent's breathing give a start, as if affected by something, and then return to its normal rise and fall. When I tug the boxers just a tiny bit more, suddenly his cock slides out of the fly, popping up as if it just burst a hole through the fabric.

His swollen, rock-hard cock ... inches from my lips.

I look up to check my victim again. Eyes still closed. Lips still parted. I listen to him breathe a few rounds before I turn my attention back to Trent's dick. *Is this really happening?* I ask myself, I ask all my dream selves who were in this situation before, who have lived this over and over again.

Except they've never really lived it. Because I'm living it. Because this is not a dream, and Trent's cock is in my face, and there are *real* consequences if he wakes up.

I've been afraid most of my life. Can't I, just this one time, be brave?

I open my mouth, daring myself. It's just right there. It's right there in front of me. *Right there.* I stick out my tongue, reaching, like an experiment.

My tongue touches the tip of his cock.

Tongue still touching, I twist my face to look up the mountain of my best friend. Eyes still closed. Mouth parted. No reaction.

I let my tongue slide. The whole pad of my tongue rests along the tip of his cock now, like the palm of a small, warm, wet hand. I dare my tongue to move.

His cock jumps.

I stop, twist my eyes to look up, frozen in place with my tongue latched on.

Eyes still closed.

I run my tongue down the length of his cock, slowly, slowly, then run my tongue back up. After seeing hundreds upon hundreds of boys do this in porn videos, it's *my turn.* I let my tongue slowly bathe every inch of his tall, swollen dick. Slowly, slowly up one side, then slowly, slowly down the other. His dick grows more and more wet, slicker, smoother as my tongue traces its length over and over and over again. He never opens his eyes.

I'm in gay heaven.

The next time I reach the tip of his cock with my tongue, I pause, taking another glance up at his beautiful, peaceful face.

Here goes nothing.

I part my lips wider and, slowly, I take his cock into my mouth.

Nerves I didn't know I had are waking up.

At first, I just accept the tip of his cock, closing my mouth around it like a popsicle. I think suddenly about Charlie and the girl he told me about on this couch, the popsicles she'd sell. *I'll take a cocksicle instead, please.*

It might be my imagination, but I think I hear his breathing quicken. I hesitate, waiting, hovering with my mouth wrapped around the tip, wondering if I should go further. *Give me a sign*, I beg him, horny, insane, desperate. *Give me any sort of sign that I can go on.*

I barely slide a bit more in, taking another *millimeter* of his cock. His breath quickens. It's not my imagination. Whether he's dreaming it or not, some part of him is aware of what's happening.

He wants it, I tell myself.

I take another inch, my tongue sliding, my wet lips sliding, his cock like a rod, firm and unrelenting and pulsing with need.

Can I satisfy that need? Me and my lips and my tongue?

Trent breathes a bit differently now, the more I take in. I hear his throat opening up, his breathing lighter, his breaths getting closer together. Trent's cock is in my mouth and his pleasure is at my mercy.

I'm in control.

The power I have with just a tongue, with just lips. If I knew I had this power before ...

I go the full length of his cock, swallowing it all. I hear him moan. *I HEAR HIM MOAN!* Fighting my gag reflex, I twist my mouth up and down his cock slowly, the entire length of him. Little Trent, pulsing, throbbing in my eager mouth.

Suddenly his hand drops from the back of the couch, lands on my head. Is he awake? I can't look up to see him, his hand now gripping the back of my head. *Oh my god*, I realize. *He woke up and he's guiding my head now. He's guiding my head on his cock.*

He wants it.

Inspired by his touch, high as a kite on the drug of want, I work his cock in my mouth with the commitment of an engine. He moans now, even louder. His breaths are raspy and quick. He's getting close, he has to be.

Just when I think he's going to shoot, something horrible and hard knocks me in the side of the head, and everything turns into dots and flashes and stars.

I'm on the floor, grabbing my head and looking up, the room spinning, confused.

"WHAT THE FUCK??" Trent screams, standing over me.

I blink away whatever it was that hit me, blink the world back into focus. "W-What?" I sound innocent. I sound confused. I sound hurt. "W-W-What happened?"

"WHAT THE FUCK!" he repeats. He doesn't put away his cock, which drips with my saliva.

I'm lost for words. Did something happen? I'm completely confused and disoriented. The room spins, my lips are wet with drool and my roommate's staring down at me with the fury of a volcano.

"I'm ... I ..." I sound so stupid. I form a sentence to say, then let it stick in my throat, terrified.

"You were sucking my dick," he says, eerily calm suddenly. He points at it, as if it's necessary to indicate what he's talking about.

I shake my head, my first impulse being to deny it all. Then, mouth hanging open stupidly, I say, "I was confused. I'm still drunk. I ... I was ..." I slap a hand to my forehead, out of words.

He doesn't say anything, frozen in place, a finger pointed at his still-hard, still-dripping dick. It still pokes out of his boxers like a middle finger, flicking me off. Even the way he's pointing at it is like flicking me off.

Fuck you, Benny. That's the message I feel like I'm getting. *Fuck you.*

"You knew what you were doing." He says it so quietly, so unsettlingly. "You were blowing me."

"I wasn't."

"You were sucking my dick."

How many more times does he have to say it? My forehead's breaking out in a sweat and my face burns redder and redder. Every time he says it, the reality of what I did becomes more real. Every time he says it, I'm more ashamed.

"I'm drunk." Despite the room spinning, I get to my feet, staggering to the left, then the right. I bring a finger to my lip, bring it into view. "I'm bleeding."

"I kneed you in the face," he mutters, and he doesn't quite sound proud of it.

Unable to meet his eyes, I stare at a thread in the couch, some thread that's been coming lose for years, some piece of that couch that's been unraveling before our eyes for years and neither of us noticed, neither of us bothered to fix it. To that thread, I say, "I'm sorry, Trent. I'm so sorry."

He doesn't say anything for a minute. I wonder if he's still pointing at his dick. *Why can't he put it away? Does he want me to finish?* I ask myself bitterly.

"So you been wantin' to do this for a while or what?" he asks.

"Fuck you, Trent."

"I'm serious, Benny."

His voice suggests he's also angry and has nothing kind to say to me right now, regardless of how I respond to his harsh interrogation.

He goes on: "You been looking at my dick when I sleep? You look at me like that?"

"No."

"I think you're lying."

"Shut the fuck up," I warn him, feeling the blood rise in my neck, the ugly blood, the kind that is *not* the stuff of passion.

"You been wantin' my junk this whole time? Your own friend? You betray my trust and you—you—you—you take advantage of your best fucking friend when he's asleep? So you can satisfy your sick perversions?"

"Shut ... the fuck ... up." My tone suggests

that it's my last warning.

"You fucking do this to your friend? You want me?—Is that it, bitch?"

I lunge across the room so fast, he barely gets his hands up in time. My fist makes a sweet friendship with his cheek, knocking him over. Having gripped my shirt, he takes me with him as he falls.

On top of him, his still-exposed cock slapping my thighs, I grapple with him on the floor. Twice we roll over ... my back slams to the floor, then his, then mine again, then his. Atop him, I throw another fist into his face just as he calls me a name.

The next punch sends a spray of blood across the floor, staining a rug my mom got us last Christmas.

When his hands come up not to attack me, but to shield his own face ... that's when I stop. I stare down at the boy I've loved for years, witnessing what I've done to him. His hands shake, ready to grab or deflect or otherwise stop the maiming my feral fists had planned. Breathing heavy, my teeth bared, I stare down at Trent, overcome, anger still billowing out of my ears, still burning my cheeks with the ugly blood.

Trent and I lock gazes, warily studying one another through sheens of tears in our quivering eyes. His blood still seasons my knuckles.

"I did," my mouth finally says, and I'm not even sure exactly what I mean. *I did want you this whole time. I did mean to suck your cock. I did take advantage of you.*

I climb off of him, finished, sick with myself. Still dressed in just a tank and gym shorts, albeit a touch roughed-up and with a speck of blood staining the tank—whether his or mine, no one can tell—I let myself out.

He might've said something. He might've called out for me, but I don't hear it.

I leave, walking down the empty street in the dead of night, joining the cacophony of crickets. A genuine wave of reluctance seizes me, threatening to turn me back home and not let me take another step, but I push through it, forcing myself recklessly into the dark.

I don't know how much time passes with these thoughts tormenting me, but I find the brick wall of a building and, almost politely, I crouch down and retch anything that's inside me. It isn't much and the most I actually do is just dry heave and groan and spit at the wall.

"I'm so sorry," I whisper to the bricks.

I half-fall, half-lean into the wall, deciding to keep my vomit company for a while, I guess. An uncharacteristic breeze wiggles down the street like a great invisible comb, sending dust into my eyes. I clench them shut and wrap my arms around my belly, hugging it tight. I better take good care of myself; I might be the only friend I got left.

After roughly half an hour of disoriented thoughts and numbness passes, I finally pull my phone out and look for my parent's number. I find Charlie's instead. When the hell did I acquire his number? Mr. Dancing Queen must've put it in there himself.

I bring the phone to my ear.

Click. "Hmmnh?"

"Ch-Charlie?" I clear my throat of phlegm or whatever the fuck builds up back there after an indeterminate amount of time spent crying and vomiting and gagging on the blood of a bleeding mouth. "Charlie?"

"Who da fuck?" I hear rustling, clothes or bed sheets or something. "Fuckin' ... 4 AM?"

"This is Benny. R-Remember me? We, umm ... We went to school together. You gave me a ride home and ... and I ..."

"It's four-the-fuck-A-M, honey. My ass needs 'ta *sleep*."

"C-Can I crash at your p-place tonight?"

There is a long silence. I pray he's actually considering it. *This is not a prank call*, I want to tell him. *I need your help. I hurt all over.*

"Where you at?" he finally asks, his tone taking a slight change for the concerned.

I have no idea. "A brick wall."

"I'll be right there."

[8]

Charlie dresses a cut above my eyebrow, a scrape on my cheek, and a gash on my knuckle with a generous assortment of Rainbow Bright Band-Aids. He offers me a shirt, but I opt to sleep shirtless instead. I remember very little else before I lay myself down on his absurdly comfortable couch, waiting for him to get me a glass of water and an Ibuprofen.

That must've been when I fell asleep.

Morning throws a blanket of piss-yellow light over my head from a window draped in pink-and-blue polka-dot curtains.

"Mornin', Sleeping Beauty," he sings from a salmon-colored armchair in the corner of the room.

I blink the light out of my eyes and twist my head. The whole room seems to twist with it. "Fuck," I groan, touching my head and discovering a puffy bandage there.

"Do I get the story now," asks Charlie, "or do I gotta make you pancakes first?"

I squint at him. I feel so hungover, the room like an aquarium of syrupy light and diffused sound. I push myself into a sitting position, feeling aches in my muscles that certainly weren't making themselves known last night, what with my rage and everything.

Rage. That's when I remember what the fuck happened last night. Trent. His dick. My misbehaving mouth. The words we threw at each other. The fist I threw into his jaw ... my best fucking friend.

"Pancakes first," I groan.

Over artful yellow-and-red plates of eggs and pancakes and chopped-up cantaloupe, I tell

Charlie the whole story. Trent and my friendship that grew into something more for me. The culmination of feelings that became my one hard and horny mistake last night. The whole story has Charlie so captivated, he doesn't interrupt once and hardly touches even the *one* tiny pancake he served himself.

When I'm finished, the most intelligent response he has is: "Wait … you're gay?"

"Yeah, whatever," I confirm with a shrug.

"Wouldn't have guessed. Shit." He pokes his pancake, looking annoyed. "If I'd known that, way back in the day, *phew* … I would 'a had my way with you, sweetheart. In the gym locker rooms. In first period and second period and every period, even my sister's, honey, I'd have taken you *everywhere and anywhere and anyway*. She had a baby last year. Girl. I'm an uncle, did you know that? Gay uncle Charlie. The baby daddy moved to Hollyweird to do gay-for-pay to afford child support. I'm a sitcom. This shit writes itself, take notes."

"Thanks for taking me in, Charlie."

Daryl Banner

"Oh, sweetie, stay as long as you want. Move the fuck in. Be *my* best friend. You can suck my cock whenever the hell you want. Saves me the hell of going to Kegs and Dregs where you only find just that: *the dregs*. Ugh. That place is sin. Did you know the owner's fucked every woman over forty in this town? He's probably fathered a fifth of our senior class. Welcome to backwater incest fuck-twat hell, it's what we live in, leave your shoes by the door, hey." He slurps his coffee, watching me over the brim of the mug. "You a virge?"

I narrow my eyes questioningly. "Virge?"

"Virgin, babe, keep up. Have you done the hocus in your pocus yet? I won't tell no one, pinky swear."

"Uh ... yeah, I guess I am." I've swallowed every bite on my plate. I could eat three times the amount he gave me, but I suck it up and appreciate the breakfast deck I've been dealt.

"Which do you think you wanna do? You the pitcher, or the lemonade? You the hot, or the sauce? I'll teach it all to you, babe."

"I'm not sure I'm in the mood to be taught nothin'," I murmur, trying not to sound too ungrateful. "Mind's a bit preoccupied with—"

"Straight boys." I nod. "Yeah, yeah. The fly in *all* our chardonnays. Trent's a cutie, I'll give him that. He's got one of those get-the-fuck-over-here-and-let-me-pinch-you sort of faces. I always wondered what it was like to kiss a guy with a lip ring." Charlie pushes his cheek into his fist, pondering exactly that. He puckers his lips, as if testing it with an imaginary volunteer before him.

"You're fuckin' weird," I can't help but blurt out, stifling a laugh.

"And really lonely."

My face turns serious, studying him. He gets up suddenly, takes both our empty plates to the sink, dumps them in loudly with the care of a barmaid.

"Me too," I say quietly.

"I'm so tired of waiting for some asshole to ride into my life to save me," he complains to the sink, his back turned. "Why is it so hard to just ... get up and take what we want? I mean, this is our fucking life. This is my life." He turns suddenly, a dishtowel with tiny pink unicorns dangling from his hand. "This is your life, you dumb mother fucker. Who told you to be quiet and careful and not get in anyone's way? What the fuck are you gonna do when you're dead, Benny? Ask for another chance? This *is* your chance. You took it. You saw Trent on the couch and you ... you sucked it. You sucked your chance, baby, and if ever the circumstance should again arrive, I say, fuck it and suck it too. Life is here for the sucking and the fucking of it, my friend. We are alive, so *be* alive."

I imagine he's waiting for the applause of an auditorium full of attendees to his self-help seminar, but all he's got is me, and my reaction is a blank stare and an unsatisfied grumble in my stomach. That, or I gotta take my morning dump already.

"I gotta get to work soon," he complains.

"Me too," I confess. "But my clothes ..."

"What is it you wear to work?—Dickies? Polo? Honey, I got it all, take your pick. I have three closets and every acceptable color of this season's and last. Have a heyday. I'm bustin' a move, bitch. Spare key's under the black dog statue. Place is yours." He leaves his mug on the counter and saunters off to the bedrooms.

He's leaving me a way in, just like that? I call after him: "You're letting me stay?"

"I'd be crazy not to. You kidding?" He stops at the hall, his butt looking tight as a rope in those jeans, his bright eyes flashing. "Didn't I just get done saying I'm a lonely mother fucker?"

My hands resting in my lap, I smile lamely. "Thanks."

"Aww, babe. Don't mention it," he says. "Like, literally, don't. I don't do sappy." He disappears into his room, the door shutting heavily at his back.

I smile, looking around and taking in the environment of his home. It's colorful and strangely inviting. I feel like I'm in some lost aunt's house, or a whacky grandma's cabin who makes rainbow-sprinkled cupcakes every Tuesday for no reason at all.

Reluctantly, I pull out my phone and look at the notifications. Trent called me an hour ago, apparently. Voicemail.

My belly somersaults. My breath goes all wrong and jagged. After steeling myself far too much, I clench my jaw and tap the button, then bring the phone to my ear, listening.

"H-Hey, uh ... hey. Just ... just calling to see where you're at or whatever. You kinda just fuckin' took off and ... and ..." He sighs loudly, a blast of static in the voicemail. "I think we should talk about this, Benny. I'd try and, like, check all your friends' houses and find out where the fuck you are ... but I know you don't got no friends but me, so ... and maybe that's the other reason why I'm, well ... why I'm fuckin' worried, I guess. Like, for real, Benny, like ... Where the f—" And the voicemail ends, cut off.

I stare at the phone, then shut my eyes.

"Spectacular," sings Charlie as he emerges from his room in a white t-shirt and skin-tight maroon pants. Sunglasses nest in his hair. "You can take whatever you want. We look about the same size, I reckon. Well, my stuff will likely squeeze you to death, but hey, tight is the new loose so, whatevs. See you after six or so. I'm ordering Chinese later, hope you like moo shu pork and lettuce wraps."

The next instant, Charlie is out the door and I'm left in a strange house with just the sound of my own unsettled digestive system for company.

I set my phone on the counter, as if afraid of it. "I'm sorry," I tell it, maybe speaking to Trent, maybe speaking to myself. I don't know anymore.

I just don't know anything anymore.

[9]

My time with Charlie is surprisingly nice. We seem to have similar work hours, though I don't quite know what he does and never bothered to ask. I like everything he orders to eat. He seems to always order delivery and never cooks. "I don't believe in stoves," he tells me. "My mother halfway cooked her boobs on one once, like in that scene in *Mrs. Doubtfire*. I'm literally afraid to bake my boobs. I don't do toasters either because every time I try to use one, my shit gets burnt."

Trent calls again Thursday afternoon.

"Aren't you ever gonna answer it?" asks Charlie after I let the phone go to voicemail. "Your girlfriend Trent is *obviously* concerned as fuck about you. He's probably posting missing persons fliers, like they do with lost puppies ..."

"He knows where I work," I say flatly. "If he really cares, he'll find me at the store."

"Oh, hey, look what I picked up." He lifts a case of beer onto the counter with the might of a lumberjack. "Your roommate's favorite. The brand I guzzled up that night I stayed at your place and almost molested you."

"I still sorta wish you had."

"That can be arranged."

It's all fun and games between us. I never know what to take seriously and what to laugh off as another of his countless jokes. But a handful of hours later when the sun's gone down, we're huddled on his couch watching reruns of *Golden Girls* and chugging beer after beer after beer. I'm squinting at the TV now and we're laughing at each other's slurring.

"You know you're really not my type at all," he tells me. "Handsome just doesn't do it for me. Believe it or not, I did *not* ogle the football team, nor did I hump to thoughts of the soccer team ... or the anything else team. The *wrestling* team, however ..."

"I peeked into one of their afterschool practices once," I confess, remembering. "The gym where they practiced was right across from my study hall, and they were all in this bent-over-backward bridge sort of position, each of them, their pelvises pointing up to the rafters. Their coach was punishing them, I think, threatening to make them hold that position for another thirty minutes if any of them fell or couldn't hold it. The dude closest to the door, bent over in a bridge in his tight blue singlet, he was sporting the biggest hard-on I'd ever seen. It was like he was *enjoying* it, but couldn't hide his enjoyment, no matter how he shifted his body or ... or anything. It was just there, out in the open, his hard-on in plain view."

"Hot," grunts Charlie. "What the fuck's your point?"

Clumsily, I push my face into his and, as if fumbling through dark woods to clasp hands with a friend, my lips latch onto his. Nothing happens, our mouths just touching, frozen together. Then, as if gently waking up, our lips begin to move, kissing one another. With growing anticipation and deepening hunger, I twist my head and bury my mouth into his as deep as I can manage. He grunts, surprised, then slowly slides to his back on the couch. I climb over him, sucking his lips and inhaling his scent.

When our lips finally part, I tell him, "You're not really my type either. But I'm a bit virge, I'm a bit lonely, and we're here and alive and all that bullshit so ... y'know, figured why the fuck not, right?"

"That's basically how it always happens," Charlie explains.

Our faces collide again. This time, Charlie takes the lead and works me onto *my* back as he climbs atop me. Ungently, he works open my shirt one stubborn button at a time. Then his mouth wanders from mine, kissing down my neck like a naughty boy taking a path in the woods he was warned against. Charlie even sneaks wicked glances up at me as he goes lower and lower, to my pec where his mouth meets a familiar friend. I clench shut my eyes and moan when his playful tongue finds my nipple again. *Yes*, I cry inside, my inner triumphant shout of victory. *A thousand times yes.*

Six billion hours of working my nipple later, he resumes his trek of kisses down my body until arriving at my pants. He pulls the belt off and throws it aside, that wicked, evil thing, then claws open my pants like branches of trees in his way.

My cock leaps out, hard as it's ever been. *Kiss it*, I beg him silently. *Lick it like I licked Trent's. Bathe it with your tongue. Oh god, I just want to know what I did to him. I want to know how it feels.*

He kisses the tip of my dick. "Yes," I say aloud, my thoughts becoming words. "Kiss it good."

Charlie follows my command. What a good boy. Those lips touch my cock with such tenderness, I feel my balls pull up tightly, my toes curl within my shoes.

"Lick it," I whisper.

When his tongue darts out, daring a taste of my cock, I gasp sharply, surprised by the sensation. *This is really happening. Finally, really, actually happening.*

"Please suck my dick." My hands grapple. I fumble blindly for his face, then find my greedy purchase in his hair. I pull him down on my dick, his warm mouth enveloping my every inch. This boy is practiced. "Fucking holy hell fuck," I blurt out.

He lifts off my cock. "You're sexier when you shut the fuck up."

I shove him back down, gagging him with my dick as I start to pump my hips. "So are you," I growl back.

My hands gripping his hair so tightly, directing him up and down my cock, I find myself licking my own lips, breathing heavier and heavier with every tongue-and-lip-assisted stroke of my cock.

I want this feeling to last forever.

"Fuck me," I say, getting close. "Oh, god, fuck, fuck me, fuck ..."

This time, he pulls completely off my cock and brings his face near mine. I almost recoil, surprised by his closeness when suddenly he asks: "Is that an invitation?"

I stammer. "I ... I meant ... I was just ..."

"Yes, right, I'm sure you were. But would you like to, Benny boy?" He grins, bites his lip. He looks halfway cute when he does that, and halfway amateur porn star idiot. "I can transport you to worlds beyond worlds, boy, with just my cock and my hands and a bottle of gooey." He grips my dick with his hand. "Pitch, or catch? Hocus, or pocus? Lemon, or lime, or take your time?"

"Just fuck me," I breathe.

A minute later, my face is pressed into a spread of five different feather pillows. My naked body feels smooth as a buttered bird on his silken sheets. I don't see him get the lube, but suddenly he's working a finger along my crack and I feel the unmistakable slickness of fuck-goo from a tube. Trent and I use it to jerk off every day.

Mmm. Trent.

"It might hurt at first, sweetie," he says from behind. "You gotta relax yourself into it. *Feel* it all. Let yourself off the edge for once. Drift, baby ... just drift away." I feel him put a finger at my hole, gently pushing. I'm so tight that I feel my hands clasp the bed sheets. Shivers run up my back. "Just drift."

"Just shut up."

I'm imagining Trent behind me working my hole instead of Charlie. My body relaxes. Charlie is being so—I mean, *Trent* is being so gentle with me. He doesn't want to hurt me. "That's it," he murmurs, though his voice is someone else's.

When his cock enters me, I don't realize it's gone in until he begins to slide in and out, his hips moving. My mouth is trapped in a perpetual jaw-drop, feeling every bit of his cock moving in and out of me. I bite the pillow and feel the slickness of his member. Is it really Trent? Is it really Charlie?

"Fuck me," I breathe. "Fuck me, fuck me, fuck me."

And he does.

The more he goes, the slicker it becomes, and the more I relax. It's a contradiction, how I'm tensing up with excitement, how it feels so fucking good, and yet I'm turning to a puddle of helpless horniness on his bed. It's like the most perfect massage in the world.

"You're tight," the person that isn't Trent says to the back of my head.

"Sorry." I groan the word, high on sex.

"Don't be. It's a fucking pleasure." He grabs my back like a horse's reins, his thighs squeezing my ass like a saddle, and he rides me into the whispers of very early morning.

But the very early morning is anything but whispers when he has me flipped over, my legs apart, and he starts to jerk me off while his cock—still hard as steel—pummels into me at full force.

"Are you ready?" he asks.

It's harder to keep up the illusion that it's Trent doing all this to me when I'm face-to-face with Charlie. But with all our sex in the air and our scents dancing like horny demons in the heat of this fast-filling room, I realize I'm with exactly the right person I need to be with and that I am not lacking.

I don't tell him I'm ready. My cock races to the brink without my permission, Charlie's expert hand making work of it. And in the sweat of his thick, warm room, I cum.

Rope after rope of transparent whiteness dresses my abs. Some of it reaches as high as my neck, a pearl necklace made of liquid fire that, on contact, turns to ice.

"You're fucking brilliant," I breathe, my eyes wide, sweat dripping down my nose.

"I *fuck* brilliantly," Charlie corrects me, his pumping having slowed after I came. "I am far from brilliant. Now it's my turn."

He pulls out, drops my legs, then straddles my stomach, half-sitting on the mess I just made across my body. He rips off the condom, tosses it across the room and, with his cock halfway to my face, he strokes himself fast.

"What's the hurry?" I ask, every muscle in my body relaxed into a state of nirvana. I reach up and throw his hands to the side. He looks down, startled. "*My* turn."

When I clasp his cock, his lips part. His eyes lock onto mine as I start to stroke his cock, gently at first, then quickening by the second.

He breathes heavy, throws his head back. His right hand, as if having a mind of its own, drifts up to his nipple. Then his left hand joins, gripping the other nipple. Squeezing, kneading, massaging them, his cock grows even harder than it was, pulsing and flexing as I jerk him off.

"Keep going, keep going, keep going," he says over and over, his thighs shaking. "Keep going, keep going."

I certainly don't stop. He's so insanely hard, I wonder if he plans to ride the edge for hours more. Surprisingly, even after cumming, I'm so into this ... The look on his face of utter bliss, even as he rocks his head back and goes into another galaxy, working his tits ...

The fantasy and the reality never align. What you tell yourself you want, and what you'll ever get, they're like strangers that will never meet. It's the lie that desperately wants to become truth. It's the straight boy in me and the fag in me. Both are truths. Both are lies. Somewhere in the middle is where I exist—where *Benny* exists, trying to convince himself who the fuck he is, but ain't no one buying it. They all see the fear in his pretty eyes. They know he's hiding something. They watch and they whisper and they wait.

Straight up, Benny. Why can't you just look them in the eye and be straight up?

"I'm cumming," Charlie warns the ceiling, squeezing his nipples red and purple.

He warns me ten times for ten minutes— once a damn minute—before finally deciding to let go of the ride, to leap off the horse, to set free the bird. And his birds fly all over my chest, one of them smacking me in the chin, another on my shoulder. Fly, birds, fly.

He falls off me like a desert-bound man off a camel's back. "Holy mackerel." The bed springs chuckle as he lands on them, bouncing.

For a good long while, the after-sex peace lays like a blanket over the room. The heat slowly dissipates, replacing itself with the coolness of air conditioning and a breeze snaking in from the cracked-open window by his purple armoire.

"You can stay here forever for all I'm concerned," says Charlie finally.

I was seconds from drifting to sleep with all this cum drying on me when he speaks, stirring me back to life. "Huh?"

"I know, I know. Trent." Charlie sighs.

We're both staring at his ceiling, sprawled out on his bed. Our legs are woven together a bit, tangled like a pile of zombie limbs, and the fingers of one of each of our hands are grazing each other like curious, playful friends. I feel strangely close to Charlie. Part of me might even entertain the idea of exploring something deeper with him, if it weren't for the apparent commitment my heart and soul has to a certain punky someone else.

"I do need to talk to him," I admit. "We do, after all, share a place. All my things are there. I'm sure he's worried about me and all that, but ..." A quivery sigh escapes my lips, thinking on that horrible night all over again. The look on his face, both before and after I punched all his blood out of it. I'd never laid a hand on him until that night.

"Sleep here tonight." He almost sounds like he's begging. "I can't be alone tonight. My soul feels all needy and crap and—Ugh, I hate feelings."

"It's too fucking late to go anyway."

"Oh, yeah. Sun's probably coming up soon, huh." He turns his head to glance at the window across from me, his eyes sparkling in the glow from the pink clock radio by the bed. "Y'know, Benny, you're actually a really good person."

Trent's bloody face looks at me in the dark, squinting at me, teary-eyed. "I'm not."

"I don't know anyone else in this town that would've come around the corner of a bar late at night to investigate a sound, happen on an obvious beating-up and bother to intervene. I might be the only proverbial torch-bearing gay in this town, but I'm not the only gay. Neither are you. We're not alone, fuckface."

"Call me fuckface again and I'll fuck your face."

He looks at me, squinting. I twist my head and shoot him a smirky smile, inspiring his face to light up. "Promise?"

Our eyes connect longer than they should, and a million unspoken thoughts seem to pass between them, like our eyes have some secret language that our mouths desperately envy. Somewhere in the space between us, yet another truth is realized.

This was just an island of relief for the two of us. It was a moment, come and gone. I'm not his type of heaven, and he's not mine. We're just two lost, lonely birds who landed on the same branch, and it's time now to flutter home.

[10]

I walk up the steps and approach my door like I'm entering a warzone. My heart's in my throat and I can't seem to make my hands work properly. Everything's slippery. I take a deep breath, my hand resting on the doorknob, and then I push it open.

No one's in the living room or kitchen. I step further inside, leaving the door open behind me. "Trent?" No one answers back. I poke my head into his bedroom, find no one there. I peer into my own. No one. I probably should've checked to see if the car was out front. Didn't even bother, figuring he'd be home. God forbid I consider that anyone else might have a life and, y'know, go out and do things.

When I return to the living room, Trent is standing at the door. I freeze in place, a deer at the first sight of the hunter. Even my breath stops. Our eyes are locked to one another's.

He speaks first, so quietly I hardly hear it. "Hey."

"Hey," I quickly return.

He doesn't say anything. Quietly, he moves to the back of the couch, then leans on it. His eyes drift to the cushions, as if he's recalling my moment of complete and utter humiliation, the moment I'll likely regret for the rest of my life.

"I don't like how this feels," I finally say, having trouble ignoring the panting of my tired heart. "I ... I hate that I hit you and ... I hate that I did ... *what I did* ... to you."

"Nah." He taps his own face, gives me a smirk. "Didn't even leave a bruise, pussy."

I break a tentative smile. "I meant ... the other stuff too. The stuff on the couch."

"I got over it," he says, shrugging. "Pretty sure I barked up the wrong tree a few times before, hittin' on girls that wanted nothing to do with me. It's basically like that." He bites his lip. He looks so cute when he bites his lip, the ring popping up.

"So what you're saying is, I'm like a girl you're way *not* into, and I barked up the wrong tree. You're calling me a girl?"

"You sure hit like one."

"I know girls who can kick your punk ass black and blue, Trent, watch out."

He grins. "Like Sandy?"

I come up to the back of the couch, leaning against it with enough space for a person between us. He doesn't flinch or move away. Somehow, that simple observation reassures me deeply. "I've been staying with ..." My heart gives a leap, worried for an instant what he'll think. "Charlie."

"I know." He picks at his fingernails.

"You found out? How?"

"News spreads. Steve and a couple of his buddies said they saw you entering Charlie's house one day after you got off work. Couple days ago, they kinda confronted me about it. I told them it didn't matter to me. Steve started saying some shitty things, so I told him his ass looked good in those jeans, and he fuckin' took off. Dipshit." Trent grins at me, his eyes finally meeting mine. "I freaked out," he says, the smile going away. "I freaked out when I woke up with a dude on my cock. I'm sorry, Benny, but I might've freaked out if you were a chick too. I didn't know what I was seeing. And then I felt hurt and betrayed and ... and a bunch of other weird shit. Believe it or not, I *am* actually surprised. I didn't fucking know. I thought ..." He reaches for the words, shaking his head. "All those times we jerked off together ... like, were you ...?"

I feel my insides squirming. "Can we not talk about that?"

"How long have ... have you ...?"

"Since ever, I guess." I cross my arms, losing the confidence I was feeling a second ago. My face is already burning.

He breathes evenly, thinking on it all. "I'm just really weirded out right now, dude. You finished food I didn't like. We, like, did the Batman and Robin thing last Halloween. We share underwear for fuck's sake."

I screw my eyes at him. "What does any of that have to do with anything?"

"It's *everything*. It's all different now. I was having one interpretation of all that and, like, you were ... you were having another." He shrugs, as if I ought to follow his logic easily. "How do I know you don't, like, sniff my underwear when I'm not home?"

"You fucking kidding me?"

"No. I have no idea. You've been my bro forever, Benny. I don't have siblings. You're it and you've been there for me and you've touched me and now you're sucking my cock."

I already feel like this is going to end in fists to face once again. "I'm the same dude."

"You are. But now that I know the truth, I'm not. I'm changed. Your truth changed me. It's all fucking changed, Benny." He crosses his arms too, tightly, shaking his head between sentences. "It's like I signed up to be your friend, to join the Benny club, and after years of being a ... participating member ... I only now notice all the fine print. If I'd known that you were *looking* at me this whole time—"

"I was drunk, Trent. You could've been anyone that night."

"Stop making excuses." He turns to face me. I meet his eyes challengingly, daring him to piss me off again. He's already halfway there. "If you want me, just say it."

"You think that's gonna solve everything? If I just come out and say that our friendship has really been a one-sided relationship this whole time? It doesn't help, Trent. I'm runnin' out of air. This town's suffocating me." My teeth are grinding through my words, whether from nerves or anger, I can't tell. "I came back to talk to you, but if ... if there's no chance of us figuring this out and going back to the way we were, then ..."

"I don't wanna go back to how it was," says Trent.

"Give me one fucking reason to stay, Trent. Give me just one, because I have about a thousand reasons to go."

"Here's one." Trent opens his arms and, despite my flinching in thinking he was about to hit me, instead his arms wrap me into a hug. He pulls me in tight, squeezing me.

Not what I was expecting, after all that.

Into my ear, he asks: "This givin' you a boner?"

"Fuck you," I say quietly, an annoyed smile breaking over my face.

"Gotta check, now. Gotta check now that everything's different," he says while he keeps holding me, speaking over my shoulder. "Hey, all those times I called you a fag ..."

"I don't care."

"I was gonna say I meant them. Each and every one, you fag. And I love you."

Fuck you, I try to say again, despite Trent's attempt to lighten things up and show me, in his straight boy punk-ass way, that he cares about me. *Fuck you* ... but the words are choked by my sudden untimely desire to spill tears.

My arms come up and suddenly I'm hugging him back, wetting his shirt with my leaky eyes.

"Like ... brother-love you," he clarifies in my ear, knowing I already know what he meant. "Not like, wanna-hump-your-ass kind of love you."

I sniffle up my tear-snot. "I know. But next time I beat you in Smash Brothers, I'm humping you so hard."

"We'll never play Smash Brothers again."

The two of us collapse into a fit of laughter, dropping to the floor and leaning up against the back of the couch, cracking the fuck up. It wasn't even that funny, but after the tension and the tears, I think we both desperately need a reason to laugh.

"I wanna reenroll," he says finally.

I lift my eyebrows. "Oh. You're leaving?"

"I wanna reenroll and ..." He bites his lip, casting his eyes to the floor. "And I think you should, too."

"Why?"

"You said it yourself. This town's fuckin' out of air, dude." He grabs my neck suddenly, pulls me into him. My head rested on his shoulder, he says, "Whether you're a homo or you're me, this town's got no one for us, and unless we get the fuck out, we're not gonna be happy. I wanna ..." He sighs. "I wanna do this *with* you, man. But I kinda want you to have your space, too. I want you to meet people. I want you to, like, suck other dicks."

I snort into his shirt. "That bad, huh?"

"Until I opened my eyes, it was heaven." He gives the side of my head a slap. "Don't you ever repeat those words."

[11]

It's our last morning to wake up in the apartment despite the majority of our stuff being packed up and shoved in the back of the car. The aroma from the pot of coffee brewing in the kitchen fills the space like a disease.

A super gay disease: "Morning, Benny," says Charlie, slurping out of Trent's favorite mug despite him distinctly telling Charlie not to. "You sleep well on that crooked-ass piece of crap you call a mattress?"

"Not everyone can have clouds for beds like you do," I spit back, sipping my milk.

Charlie grins, scrolling through his phone with his free hand. "I'm a bit excited about this acting class we're taking with Professor Kozlowski." He slurps on his coffee again. "Can we do a scene together? Let's do a gritty sexy scandalous scene together."

"I only agreed to take that class because I needed the fine arts credit," I warn him. "I'm going for business and psychology. I'm taking over my pop's store someday, or maybe opening my own."

"Puh-leeze." Charlie sets down his mug and leans over the counter, getting up in my space. "Dream bigger, bub. You're going to be a college boy, soon. Ain't no way in hell we're coming back to this hellhole, so you better get yourself some ideas and fashion yourself a future. Build an empire. Invent a fuck-what. What's a fuck-what? I don't know, but you're gonna invent it and make millions. Hey." He lays a kiss on my cheek, pops me in the ear. "Maybe you'll meet a sexy man or two along the way."

Just in time, Trent emerges from the door, coming back into the apartment from lugging the last box downstairs. He's dressed in a smart button shirt and slacks, a chain hanging from his pocket. "Sup, boys," he says, then notices Charlie and the mug. "What the fuck."

"It's our last morning here," Charlie spits back, rolling his eyes. "Your ass wasn't gonna drink my high-dollar coffee anyway."

Trent smirks. "Point taken. Car's packed and ready to go, boys."

His piercing eyes meet mine. I've come a long way since that tumultuous time when I sucked his cock and nearly ruined everything. He's also come a long way, having apologized at least seven times for "overreacting" and then having to convince me that, while he's not gay, he might be open to getting drunk enough to let that happen again. I smirked and told him some hotter fuck was waiting for me at the university and he missed his chance.

Of course, hearing that from Trent made me swell with a certain dark pride.

"Finish up that high-dollar shit," Trent tells Charlie, giving him a nod. "I'm ready to blow this joint and get the fuck to campus. Nine hour drive. Hope you guys brought good music on those phones. Mine's still broken."

Charlie's about to enthusiastically mention his discography from gay hell when I say, "I got the music covered. Charlie, don't even think about it."

Charlie smirks. "Y'all fools got no taste." He goes back to his phone, scrolling and checking things while finishing his coffee.

I turn to face Trent. His eyes look glassy, far away. I know that look. Coming up to him, I grip his shoulders and give him a rub. "It's gonna be fine, man."

"I know. I'm good."

"Nah, you're not." I whack him on the head, give his shoulder a shake. "It's nerve-wracking, I know. Long drives into our possibly radically-changed futures can be a bit of a mind-freak-out. But we got each other, buddy. We can do this."

"I know. Alright." He takes a deep breath, lets it all out in my face. "Sorry."

"Fuck. You need a mint."

Trent smiles, adorable as ever, his lip ring popping and his eyes sparkling. "You do realize you're the inspiration behind this whole thing, right? Like, I'm pretty sure if I didn't have you in my life, I'd still be sitting on that couch playing fuckin' ... games until my thumbs turned to bone."

"Look at us," I say, picking up his muse. "We're still together. Look at all the shit we've gotten through."

"All the shit we've yet to get through."

"It's just a nine hour drive." I shake his shoulders again, bringing his adorable face back to mine. "A nine hour drive and then we're fuckin' free."

I finally see the first bits of fear vanish from his eyes, replaced with a twisted sort of courage. "We're gonna get ourselves some fuckin' degrees."

"And a life, maybe," I jest.

"Hey!" shouts Charlie. "You two bromos finished makin' out over there? I just made nine playlists, one for each hour, and we got a big ol' campus to corrupt. Things to do, people, things to do."

I grab my bag off the couch, sling it over a shoulder. "Let's get the fuck out."

"Say goodbye." Trent gives the place a kiss in the air, then slaps the wall and swings out the door.

After Charlie gives the apartment a wiggle of his fingers and hops down the stairs, I'm the last to leave. Looking back at the place, my eyes come to rest on the couch.

With just the sight of it, I feel the warm embrace of imaginary Trent, the one that kept stealing his way into my dreams, and the brave and wicked imaginary Benny who let it all happen, who lived the fantasies that I could never know.

I think about all the things I said to Trent and all the things I didn't. All the things that imaginary Benny could do and say.

My heart swells up. "Goodbye," I tell them both, whether the imaginary ones that loved each other straight up, or the real ones.

The end.

Made in the USA
Lexington, KY
04 June 2018